BRANDYWINE PUBLIC SCHOOLS
Elementary Library
2428 S. 13th Street
Niles, MI 49120

BRANDYWINE PUBLIC SCHOOLS
Elementary Library
2429 S. 13th Street
Niles, MI 49120

GEOGRAPHY
OF THE SOVIET UNION

Read for accuracy by

Series Consultant
David McDonald
Professor of History
University of Wisconsin—Madison

Copyright © 1989 Raintree Publishers Limited Partnership

All rights reserved. No portion of this book may be reproduced or utilized in any form or by any means, electronic or mechanical, including photocopying, recording, or by any information storage and retrieval system, without permission in writing from the Publishers. Inquiries should be addressed to Raintree Publishers, 310 West Wisconsin Avenue, Milwaukee, Wisconsin 53203.

Library of Congress Number: 89-3680

1 2 3 4 5 6 7 8 9   94 93 92 91 90 89

Library of Congress Cataloging-in-Publication Data

Clark, James I.
  Geography of the Soviet Union / James I. Clark.
  (Portrait of the Soviet Union)
  Includes index.
  1. Soviet Union—Description and travel—1970-   —Juvenile literature.
I. Title. II. Series: Clark, James I.   Portrait of the Soviet Union.
DK29.C59   1989   914.7—dc19   89-3680
ISBN 0-8172-3353-9 (hardcover)
ISBN 0-8172-3363-6 (softcover)

Cover Photo: TBS/Reagan

GEOGRAPHY OF THE SOVIET UNION

James I. Clark

RAINTREE PUBLISHERS
Milwaukee

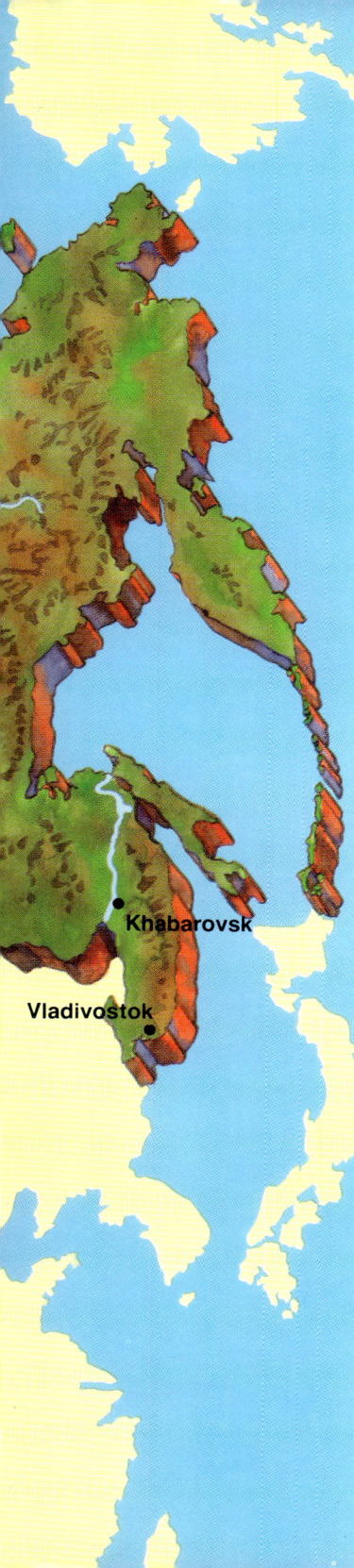

CONTENTS

Introduction	6
LAND REGIONS	**8**
The European Plain	8
The Ural Mountains	10
The West Siberian Plain	12
The Central Siberian Plain	12
The East Siberian Uplands	13
Soviet Central Asia	14
CLIMATE	**16**
Climatic Regions and Precipitation	18
VEGETATION ZONES	**20**
The Tundra	20
The Taiga	22
The Steppe	24
The Deserts	24
Subtropical	26
USING NATURAL RESOURCES	**27**
Humans and Tundra	28
The Taiga	30
Farming	30
Organization of Farming	33
Resources for Industry	36
TRANSPORTATION	**38**
POPULATION	**43**
A Chronology of the Soviet Union	46
Map of Soviet Republics	47
Index	48

INTRODUCTION

Imagine walking across part of Europe and all of Asia! Georgyi Busheyev not only imagined it, according to the *Guinness Book of World Records,* he did it.

During 1973-1974, Georgyi Busheyev spent 238 days walking from Riga, the capital of the Latvian Soviet Socialist Republic, to Vladisvostok, on the Pacific Ocean. His journey took him through cities, towns, and villages. He crossed rivers and streams and mountain passes and grasslands, and he skirted the shores of lakes. Altogether, Busheyev tramped more than 6,000 miles (9,650 kilometers). He saw much more geography than most people read about. Still, he observed only a small portion of the Union of Soviet Socialist Republics (U.S.S.R.), the largest country in the world.

Vast is the only word to describe the Soviet Union. Its area is 8,649,489 sq. miles (22,402,073 sq. km). West to east, it measures the distance Georgyi Busheyev covered. North to south, the distance is 3,200 miles (5,150 km). The country's coastlines altogether run 30,787 miles (49,547 km). And it has been estimated that by the mid-1990s, the Soviet Union's population will be approximately 300 million.

Ossetia, in the Caucasus. These huts are ossuaries, housing the bones of the dead.

A lone child plays on a Baltic beach.

LAND REGIONS

The outstanding thing about Soviet Union geography is its general flatness. A large part of the country is made up of plains—the European Plain and the Western Siberian Plain. These plains—called steppes—are two of the six geographical regions into which the Soviet Union might be divided.

The European Plain

To the southwest, the Carpathian Mountains form part of the western border of the European Plain. The Carpathians are old, worn-down mountains. They have few peaks that rise higher than 6,000 feet (1,800 meters).

High mountains mark part of the southern boundary of the European Plain. These are the Caucasus. They run for about 750 miles (1,210 km) from the northwest to the southwest between the Black Sea and the Caspian Sea. Their highest peak is Mount Elbrus, at 18,481 feet (5,633 m). This is also the highest peak in Europe.

The European Plain itself is gently rolling land, crisscrossed by many rivers and streams. The Volga River is the longest of the region. It flows 2,194 miles (3,531 km) from the Valdai Hills, near Moscow, to the Caspian Sea in the south.

Many tributaries—such as the Oka, Kama, Vetluga, and Sura—flow into the Volga. The entire river system drains an area of 525,000 sq. miles (1.3 million sq. km). The Volga is frozen along much of its length during three months or more every year.

The names of five other rivers on the European Plain begin with the letter "D." They are the Dniester, the Dnieper, the Don, and two

The rugged Caucasus Mountains rise to form the western border of the European Plain.

Dvinas.

Rising in the Carpathian Mountains, the Dniester River passes through the southwestern corner of the European Plain. After flowing 877 miles (1,411 km), the Dniester reaches the Caspian Sea.

Like the Volga, the Dnieper rises in the Valdai Hills. However, it flows southwest through the city of Kiev and then south and west to the Black Sea. The Dnieper is 1,420 miles (2,285 km) long.

A small lake near Tula, south of Moscow, forms the headwaters of the Don River. This river is 1,224 miles (1,970 km) long. The Don flows south from the lake, and then west to the Sea of Azov. The two Dvina rivers are the Western Dvina and the Northern Dvina. The Western flows north from near Moscow for 633 miles (1,019 km) to empty into the Gulf of Riga. The Northern Dvina is 824 miles (1,326 km) long. It begins in foothills of the Ural Mountains and moves north into the White Sea near the city of Arkhangelsk.

The Ural Mountains

Forming a land region themselves, the Ural Mountains border the European Plain on the east. They run south from near the Arctic Ocean toward the Caspian Sea.

The rolling plains outside Volgograd.

The Urals were formed 225 million years ago, and today they are little more than rounded hills from about 1,000 to 6,000 feet (300 to 1,800 m) high. They average about 2,000 feet (600 m) in height. The highest peak is Mount Narodnaya, 6,214 feet (1,894 m) in elevation.

The West Siberian Plain

The West Siberian Plain is the largest plains region in the world. It covers more than one million sq. miles (2.6 million sq. km). No place on the plain is higher than 500 feet (152 m) above sea level.

Among the region's rivers, the Ob-Irtysh waterway is the most important. Both rivers rise in the Alta Mountains, along the Chinese-Mongolian border in the south. Both flow in a northwesterly direction. The rivers join at the cities of Khanty and Mansiyusk. They then course toward the north into the Kara Sea, part of the Arctic Ocean. Together, the Ob-Irtysh system is 3,362 miles (5,411 km) long.

During much of the year, the northern reaches of the Ob-Irtysh are frozen, and the ice breakup occurs earlier in the south than in the north. This causes ice jams and flooding. Because the region is so level, water does not run off. Swamps and marshes form over much of the land.

The Central Siberia Plateau

The Yenisey River rises in the Sayan Mountains, northwest of the Alta, and also empties into the Kara Sea. This river forms the boundary between the West Siberian Plain and the Central Siberian Plateau. It is 2,543 miles (4,093 km) long. The region extends east to the Verkhoyansk Mountains and south to the Sayan and Baikal mountains. The hundreds of streams running through the region have cut deep gorges and canyons in the plateau.

Lake Baikal is the outstanding feature of the southern part of the Central Siberian Plateau. This lake, which formed 25 million years ago, is the deepest freshwater lake in the world. In fact, it contains one-fifth of the entire earth's supply of fresh water. More than six hundred different plants and twice that many animal species are found in and around the lake. For example, the world's only freshwater seals live there.

Baikal is 395 miles (636 km) long and 50 miles (80 km) wide. It covers an area of 12,152 sq. miles (31,474 sq. km). Its deepest point is 5,315 feet (1,620 m)—more than a mile. A total of 336 rivers flow into the lake. Only one flows out of it.

The Lena River, one of the longest in the U.S.S.R., flows out of the Baikal Mountains and north to the Laptev Sea, part of the Arctic

Ocean. The Lena is 2,734 miles (4,400 km) long.

The East Siberian Uplands

The East Siberian Uplands is the Soviet Union's largest region. It is often called the Soviet Far

TASS/SOVFOTO

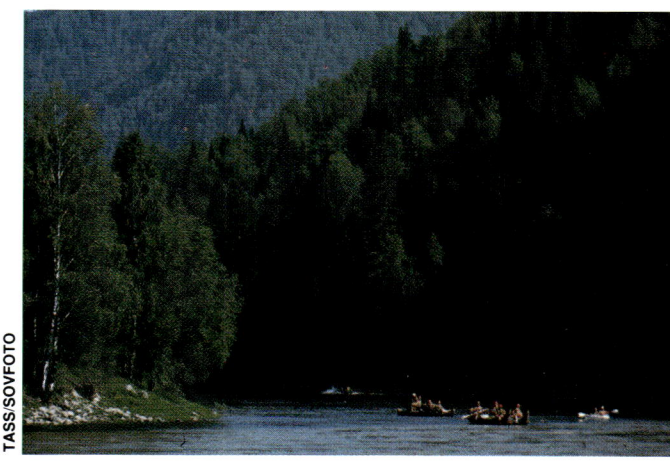

Right: *tourists raft on the Yenisei. This river forms a border between the Central Siberian Plateau and the West Siberian Plain.* Below: *Lake Baikal.*

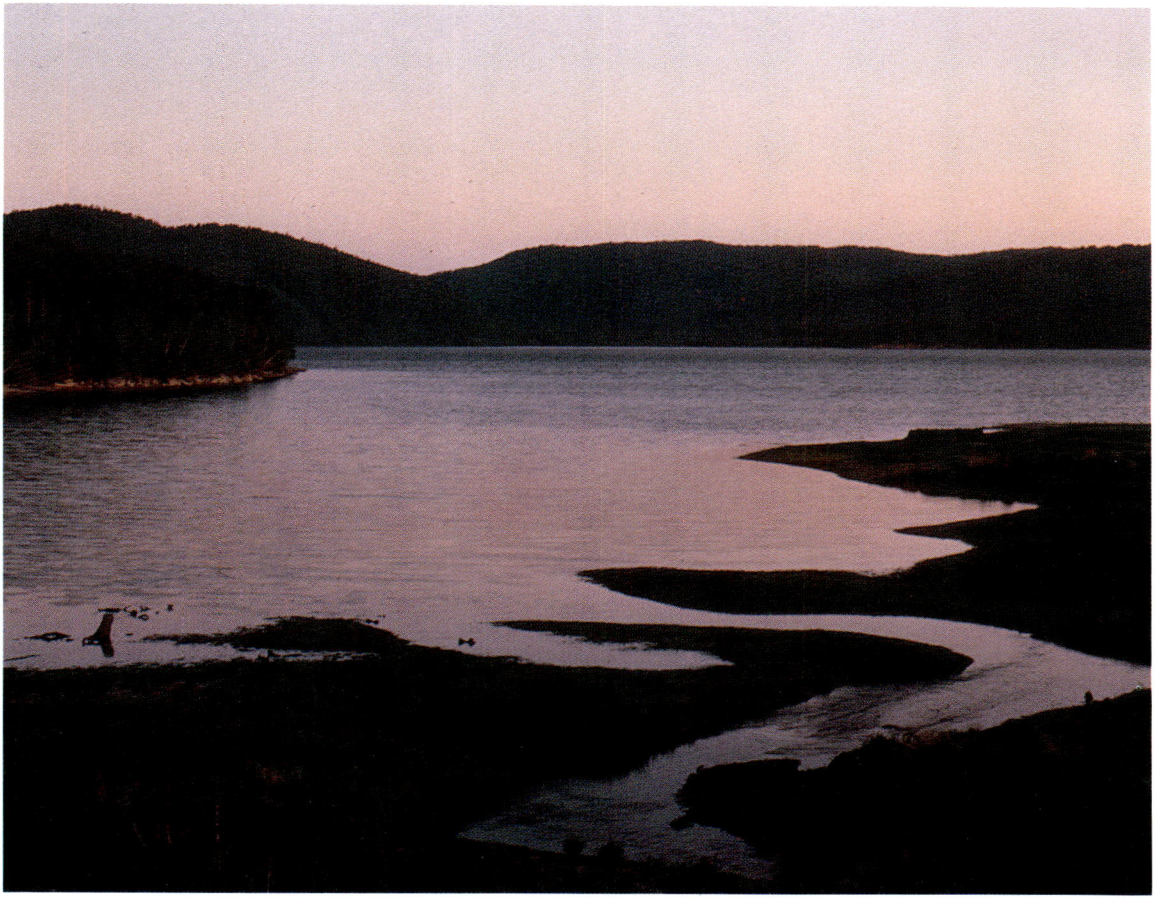

TBS/Reagan

A cloud of steam hangs over the crater of this volcano on the Kamchatka Peninsula in eastern Siberia.

East. China borders much of it on the south. To the east is the Pacific Ocean and to the north, the Arctic Ocean.

Most of the region is mountainous, with peaks rising as high as 10,000 feet (3,050 m). Much of the land is wilderness.

Part of the region is the Kamchatka Peninsula, which separates the Pacific Ocean from the Sea of Okhotsk. The peninsula contains many hot-water geysers that erupt with spray on regular schedules. The twenty-five or more active volcanoes on the peninsula are far less predictable.

The Amur River marks the southern boundary of the East Siberian Uplands, and the border between the Soviet Union and China. The Amur is 2,744 miles (4,416 km) long. It turns north into Soviet territory at the city of Khabarovsk.

Soviet Central Asia

Soviet Central Asia lies to the south of the West Siberian Plain. It stretches 1,150 miles (2,170 km) from the Caspian Sea to the Chinese border. Most of the land lies at or below sea level. It is also a region of immense deserts where rivers dry up, and of low, grassy plateaus.

Within Soviet Central Asia are the lowest and the highest elevations in the Soviet Union. The Karagiye Depression, 433 feet (132 m), lies near the Caspian Sea. In the Pamirs mountain system, along the southern border, Communism Peak rises 24,590 feet (7,495 m) above sea level. Fedchenko Glacier, also found in the Pamirs, is one of the longest valley glaciers in the world. It stretches for 44 miles (71 km).

Soviet Central Asia borders the Caspian Sea, and so does the European Plain. The Caspian is actually a great salt lake lying 92 feet (28 m) below sea level. It is about 750 miles (1,210 km) long and from 130 to 300 miles (209 to 483 km) wide. Altogether the Caspian Sea covers 143,244 sq. miles (371,000 sq. km). It is the largest inland body of water in the world.

Important rivers that drain into the Caspian Sea include the Volga, the Ural, and the Kura. Over the centuries, the sea has been shrinking in size. The rivers flowing into it provide less water than is lost each year by evaporation.

The saltiest part of the Caspian Sea is the Gulf of Kara-Bogaz, lo-

The domed houses and mosque of the Uzbek city of Khiva in Soviet Central Asia.

cated on the eastern side. It is about 37 miles (60 km) wide and 14.8 feet (4.5 m) at its deepest point. Water enters the gulf through a narrow channel shaped like the neck of a bottle. The water churns like that of a rapids in a river. It boils like water in a kettle as the desert sun heats it, causing a great deal of evaporation. Pure white salt piles up on the beaches of the gulf, making them look as though they were covered with snow.

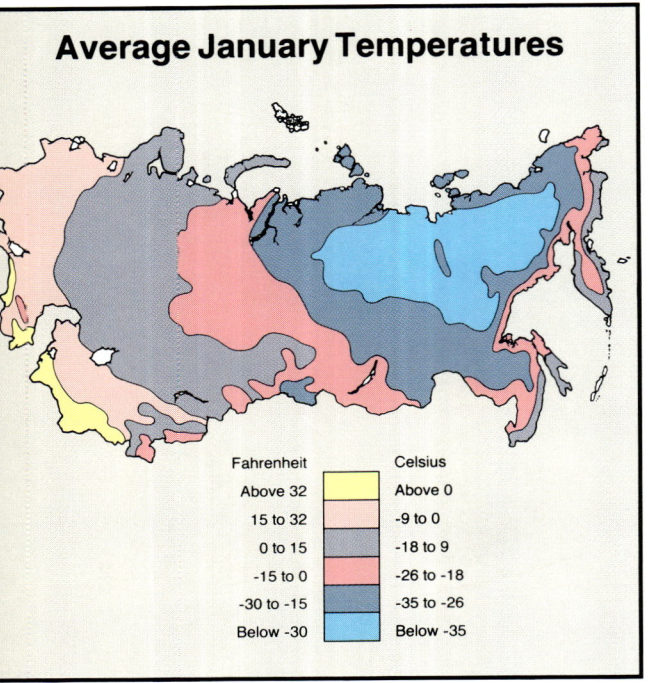

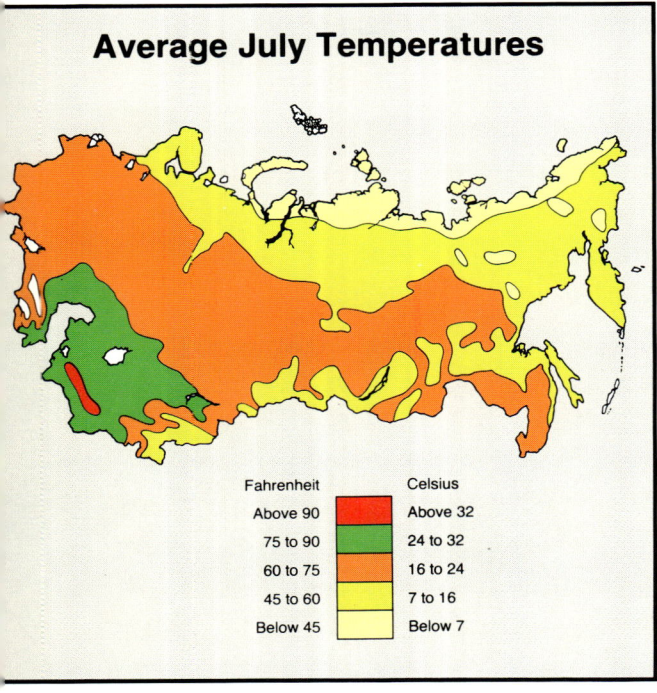

CLIMATE

No visitor to what is now the Soviet Union has failed to note the climate of that land. Five hundred years ago, a visitor from England had this to say:

"Winter and summer are much different here. In the winter the whole country lies under snow, which falls continually. It is sometimes a yard or more deep, and even deeper toward the north. The rivers and other waters are frozen up to a yard or more thick, no matter how swift or broad they may be. This continues for at least five months, from November to about the end of March, when the snows begin to melt.

"It makes a person feel frosty just to look around and see the winter face of this country. The sharpness of the air you may judge by this: if water is dropped or thrown up in the air, it freezes before it hits the ground. In winter, if you hold a pewter dish or pot in your hand, your fingers will freeze to it, and pull off the skin when you try to release it. When you move from a warm room into a cold one, your breath stiffens, and the cold makes you hurt as you breathe in and out. The winter cold can make people lose the tips of their noses and ears, their toes, and even the roundness of their cheeks to frostbite.

"Yet summer is so much different. The woods, mostly birch and fir trees, are fresh and sweet, and the pastures and meadows are green. A great variety of flowers and songs of birds suddenly burst out. No country could be more pleasant.

"As the sun warms the land and melts the snow, the land is watered, and heat from the sun draws plants from the soil in great plenty and variety and in a very short time. Summer, though, tends to be overly hot, especially the months of June, July, and August."

Things have not changed in five hundred years. The average temperature in January in Moscow ranges from 0° to 15° Fahrenheit (-18° to -9° Celsius), and below -30°F (-34°C) in Yakutsk, on the Lena River in east-central Siberia. The area around Yakutsk recorded the lowest temperature ever in the Northern Hemisphere: lower than -90°F (-68°C). Summer temperatures in Moscow range from 60° to 75°F (16° to 24°C). In Yakutsk the range is not much different.

In the Soviet Union, winter is a time of preparation, especially in Siberia. Buildings are constructed with thick walls and two or three panes of window glass. Buildings also have two or three doors at every entrance. Automobile engines are often not powerful enough to operate in very cold weather, and truck and bus engines must be run every other hour or so when not in use. Most have double windshields with a sealed air space between to prevent frosting and fogging. Railroad locomotive engines are seldom shut down, and great care must be taken to keep track switches from freezing. Airplanes operate without much trouble during the winter, but because their doors become locked in frost during flight, they must be defrosted with jets of steam before people can leave the planes.

Pipes above ground carrying drinking water to buildings in Siberia must be heated every few feet to keep the water from freezing. Sometimes water is delivered to buildings in the form of chunks of ice sawed from frozen rivers. Milk might be sold by the frozen chunk, to be carried home like a large brick. Freezers are not needed in winter. A family has only to hang food in a bag outside a window, bringing pieces in to thaw as they are needed.

Climatic Regions and Precipitation

Generally speaking, the Soviet Union features long, cold winters and short, hot summers. It has what is called a continental climate. This means that much of the land is far from any large body of water, such as an ocean, that might have an influence on the climate. For example, Bergen, Norway, is about the same distance from the equator as Moscow. Yet the differences in the two cities' climates are great. January temperatures in Moscow average from 0° to 15°F (-18° to -9°C). In Bergen they range from 27° to 43°F (-3° to 6°C). July temperatures in Moscow average from 60° to 75°F (16° to 24°C). In Bergen they range from 51° to 72°F (11° to 22°C). Bergen lies on the Atlantic Ocean, and air from the ocean tends to cool the land in summer and warm it in winter. Moscow, on the other hand, lies far inland from a body of water. The Atlantic Ocean also brings a great deal of precipitation to Bergen. The yearly average is 80 inches (203 centimeters). Moscow gets 20 to 30 inches (50 to 75 cm) of precipitation each year.

Even though the U.S.S.R. overall has a continental climate, there are differences in climate within such a huge land. They range from a polar climate in the north to a desert climate in certain areas in the south.

Snow and below-freezing temperatures are found in the polar region, on a strip of land in the north running along the Arctic Ocean. South of there is a broad area of subarctic climate. Here winters are extremely cold, and summers are short and chilly. Farther south, in the western part of the Soviet Union, the climate is moist continental. That is, winters are cold, but summers are warm to cool. Then comes a strip of steppe, or grasslands, where the weather is cold in winter and in summer quickly changes from hot to cold as night approaches. Winter is not severe in the desert region south of the steppe. Days are hot and nights are cold, however, and there is very little rainfall at any time.

Two small areas along the Black Sea have a climate much like that along the Mediterranean Sea. Summers are warm, and winter temperatures are usually above freezing. Rain falls during the winter, and summers are dry.

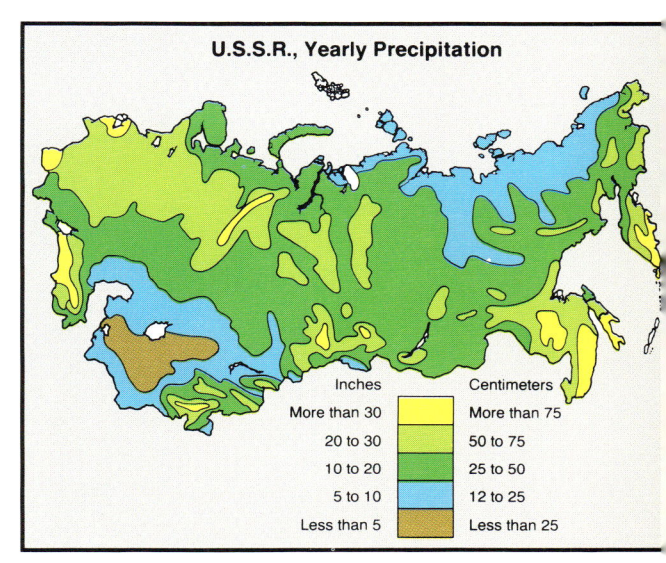

The summer temperature in Uzbekistan often soars above one hundred degrees. Here, two friends cool off at a public fountain in Khiva.

TBS/Reagan

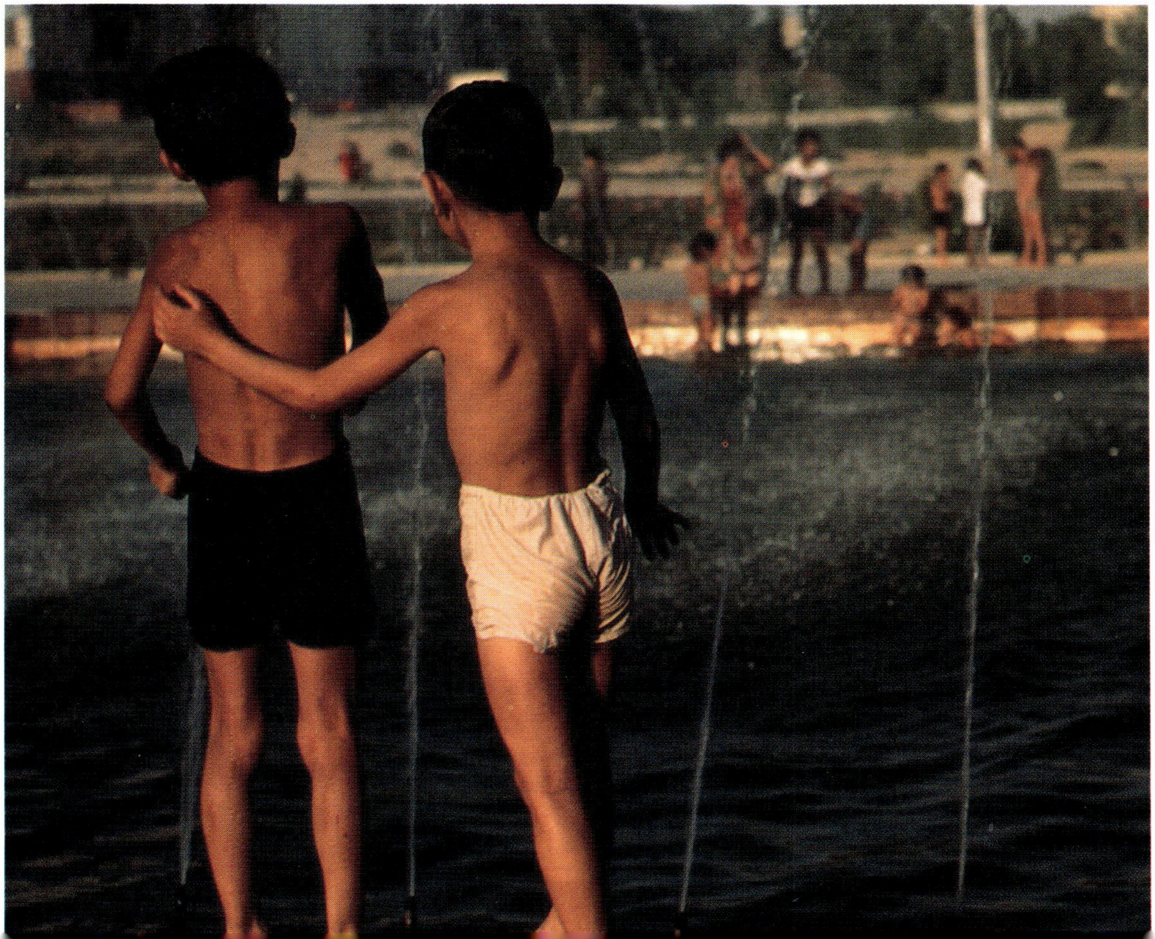

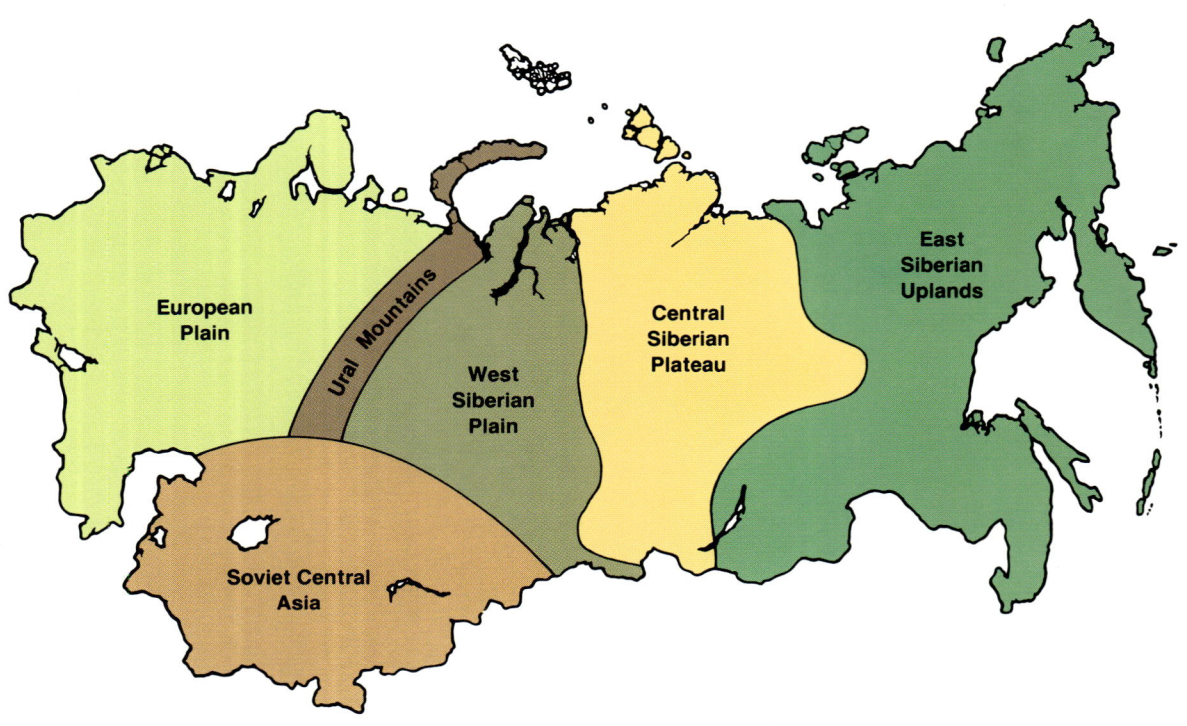

Land Regions of the Soviet Union

VEGETATION ZONES

As the climate changes from north to south in the Soviet Union, so does plant and animal life. The land can be divided into five zones. Four range from the ice and cold of the Arctic in the north to the hot, desert regions of the south. These zones are the tundra, taiga, steppe, and desert. The fifth and smallest is called subtropical, or Mediterranean zone.

The Tundra

The tundra is a treeless plain running along the Arctic Ocean and including islands in that ocean. The region extends south to where July temperatures average 50°F (10°C), where trees will grow. The tundra covers about 850,000 sq. miles (2.2 million sq. km).

Temperatures in the tundra average far below freezing for nine months of the year. From December 23 to March 21, the sun does not rise above the horizon. The hands of a clock might show that it is noon. Even so, day after day in midwinter, there will be no natural light outside at that time.

In addition, the land may be shrouded in fog or under blizzard conditions as high winds hurl stinging flakes of snow. The yearly precipitation, all snow, amounts to about 5 to 10 inches (12 to 25 cm). The tundra is more a land of ice than snow.

Beneath the surface, the land lies frozen to a depth of 1,000 feet (305 m) or more. This permanently frozen subsoil is called permafrost.

Little wildlife may be seen on the tundra during the winter. There are occasionally small bands of reindeer, lemmings scurrying from one hold to another, and now and then a polar bear or an arctic fox or hare. Gyrfalcons and snowy owls—birds of prey—along with rock ptarmigans also make the tundra their winter home.

The contrast between the dreary, dark winter on the tundra and the short summer is dramatic. By June, the sun is on the horizon and there is no night. Temperatures rise toward 50°F (10°C). Snow and ice melt. Even the permafrost thaws to a depth of about 2 feet (.6 m). This creates pools of water and areas of swamp. Stretches of moss-covered soil turn from brown to green as small plants burst into flowers of many colors. At the same time, birds of all kinds, shapes, and sizes invade the land from the south. There are ducks, geese, swans, pipits, snow buntings, snipes, ruffs, and many others. There are also immense

Rapid spring snowmelt thaws the tundra and permits a brief summer flowering.

swarms of flies and mosquitoes to plague all other living creatures. The swarms are thick enough to block out the sun.

By August, the days have grown short once again. The flowers are gone. Flocks of birds rise up each day to migrate south. Winter silence soon takes over the land.

Small clumps of trees appear along the southern edge of the tundra zone. The landscape gradually turns into the *taiga*, a Russian word meaning "thick forest."

The Taiga

This band of continuous forests runs for 5,000 miles (8,050 km) from east to west, nearly the entire width of the Soviet Union. North and south, the region varies from 600 to 1,200 miles (965 to 1,930 km). A portion of the eastern part of the taiga extends to the southern border of the U.S.S.R. The whole region covers an area of about 3 million sq. miles (7.8 million sq. km).

Winters are long and cold in the taiga region, but there are no periods of complete darkness, as on the tundra. High temperatures in the summer in much of the region range between 60° and 75°F (16° to 24°C). Precipitation on the average amounts to 10 to 20 inches (25 to 50 cm) a year. In the northern part of the region, the melting of the permafrost in summer allows tree roots to soak up

The Ingoda River, in the Chita region of Siberia, saws through the eastern reaches of the taiga.

moisture.

Larch, along with pine, spruce, and fir, are the main trees over much of the taiga. In some areas, the trees are so dense that little sunlight reaches the ground. As a result, rainfall does not easily evaporate. Drainage is poor, and the land is a spongelike bog.

The taiga abounds in animal life. Brown bear, beaver, sable, fox, lynx, vole, and squirrel are found there. There is also a great variety of birds.

West of the Ural Mountains is a peak of hardwood forest. This part of the taiga forms a triangle whose base extends to the western border

Horses are still used to drag the haywains on this Moldavian collective.

of the Soviet Union.

Such trees as oak, elm, and maple grow there, along with birch and beech. Much of the hardwood forest has been cut down to provide space for farmland and the growth of cities.

The Steppe

The wooded region gradually gives way in the south to yet another vegetation zone. This is the steppe, which in Russian means "plains." This level region runs for 1,000 miles (1,609 km) or more from Kazakhstan in Central Asia west to the western borders of the Moldavian and Ukrainian republics and along the borders of the Black Sea. The soil of the steppe is chernozem—"black earth." This is one of the most fertile soils in the world.

To the east, the steppe is semi-arid, covered with short grass. This is an ideal grazing region. Precipitation is greater in the western portion. In some places it is higher than 30 inches (76 cm) per year. The plants that grow in the western steppe include grains, sugar beets, tobacco, and flax.

The Deserts

A narrow band of semiarid land runs along the southern border of the steppe region. South of there, and east of the Caspian Sea in Central Asia are true deserts. They extend to the mountain regions that form the southern boundary of the Soviet Union.

Less than 8 inches (20 cm) of precipitation fall each year. Desert summers are the longest and hottest in the U.S.S.R. Ground temperatures as high as 176°F (80°C) have been recorded. Some species of cacti, along with sand sedge and meadow grass, survive there. Beetles, reptiles, small ro-

The steppe holds the most fertile soil in the U.S.S.R. This region has been called "the breadbasket of Russia."

Shelter belts of trees are planted to help control sand erosion in the Kara Kum.

dents, and the two-humped Bactrian camel also reside there.

The desert called Kara Kum—or "black sands"—covers 72,760 sq. miles (188,448 sq. km) between the Caspian Sea and the Amu Dayra River. A large part of Kara Kum is made up of loose sands, sandy hills, and dunes shifted by the wind. The sands of Kara Kum are called black, although actually they are whitish gray in color. Below the surface is rich, dark soil, which accounts for the coloring. *Kara* can also mean "fertile," in the Turkmen language. Kara Kum is very fertile when spring rains soak the desert. For a few weeks, many areas burst into spectacular color. Hardy plants that are well adapted to such a hot, dry climate almost suddenly bloom with flowers.

Northeast of Kara Kum is Kyzyl Kum, with an area of 81,000 sq. miles (209,789 sq. km). This desert lies between the Amu Darya and the Syr Darya rivers. Both of them flow from southern mountains into the Aral Sea. *Kyzyl Kum* means "red sands" in the Turkmen language, and in this case the name is suitable. The sands are light rose in color.

North of the Aral Sea is another arid region, the Aralian Desert. This is smaller than Kara Kum and Kyzyl Kum.

The Aral Sea, like the Caspian, is a body of salt water. It is 270 miles (435 km) long, 175 miles (282 km) wide, and from 55 to 223 feet (17 to 68 m) deep. The total area of the Aral Sea is 25,660 sq. miles (66,459 sq. km).

Subtropical, or Mediterranean

Finally, there are two areas that make up the subtropical, or Mediterranean zone. One is located along the western shore of the Black Sea. This is a narrow strip of land with the Caucasus Mountains in the background. The other area is the southern part of the

Crimean Peninsula, which thrusts into the northern part of the Black Sea to form the Sea of Azov.

These zones have warm climates with rainy winters and dry summers. Citrus trees and date trees grow well there.

USING NATURAL RESOURCES

One might expect that such a vast country as the Soviet Union would be blessed with many natural resources, and this is indeed the case. About 5.5 million acres (2.2 million hectares) of land can be farmed. Within its borders, the U.S.S.R. has nearly every mineral resource useful to humans. It leads the world in the production of iron ore, coal, oil and natural gas, diamonds, and gold. The nation's huge forests make it a leading producer of wood and wood products. Its forests also contain many animals whose furs are valuable, such as sable, silver and black fox, and mink. These are also raised on "fur farms." The Soviet Union's rivers, lakes, and coastal waters teem with fish. Huge dams provide water

Two uses of Soviet water resources: a fishing boat on Lake Bolshiya (above) and a hydroelectric generating plant at a dam on Lake Baikal (right).

power to generate billions of kilowatt hours of electricity. Reservoirs behind dams provide water for irrigation.

Climate, however, has a great effect on the use of natural resources. In many areas in the U.S.S.R., the growing season is scarcely three months long. The lack of moisture at the right time reduces the amount of food that might be grown. At other times, there might be too much moisture. Even though the soil might be fertile, in certain areas crops can be raised only with irrigation. Although mineral resources are abundant, many are located in areas such as the far north, where human living is extremely difficult.

Humans and the Tundra

At one time few humans spent more than the brief summer period on the tundra. Lapps, Inuits, Samuyds, Chukchis, and Nenets—all natives of northern lands—visited the tundra in summer to herd reindeer or to gather skins, meat, bones, and oil from animals such as seals. As winter came on, these nomadic people retreated south to the taiga region.

The tundra is rich in mineral resources, and today more than one million people live there. Most of them are Russians and Ukrainians. The city of Murmansk, where about one-half million people live, is the main center of population. Murmansk is a young city, only about eighty years old.

Murmansk is also a seaport, located far north of the Arctic Circle. Winters are long and hard, and there are days of darkness. Despite its location, though, the Murmansk harbor is free of ice all year long because of the Gulf Stream. This is a current of warm water that flows out of the Gulf of Mexico north and east across the Atlantic Ocean. It curves around Norway and Sweden into the Barents Sea, on which Murmansk is located.

More than fifteen thousand of the people in Murmansk make their living by fishing. Fishing fleets sail far from home on voyages that last five months or longer. The catches they return with keep around five thousand people at work in fish canneries. In addition, Murmansk is a center for shipbuilding and the production of wood products. The Polar Research Institute of Marine Fish-

A herdsman grazes his reindeer on the tundra in eastern Siberia's Koryak districk.

eries and Oceanography is located in Murmansk.

People are attracted to such places as Murmansk because they can earn higher pay than in Moscow or other more southern cities. They get more than forty days vacation a year. In addition, every three years, they may have a round-trip ticket to anywhere in the U.S.S.R. they choose to go.

East of Murmansk, Norilsk is located inland from the Arctic Ocean on the Pyasina River. It is a city of about 200,000 people. Norilsk is a center for smelting nickel, copper, and cobalt. These minerals are mined northeast of Norilsk, around the new town of Snezhnogorsk, on the Tamur Peninsula.

Great fields of oil and natural gas have been found in the southern portion of the Yamal Peninsula, which juts into the Kara Sea. Natural gas is piped from there to Leningrad.

Although large supplies of food must be brought in to feed the populations of the Arctic region, certain foods are produced there. Reindeer farms furnish meat as well as hides. Experiments have been conducted to heat the outdoor soil during the short growing season of two months or so to grow such foods as potatoes, cabbage, and vegetables. In addition, heated greenhouses are also used for food production.

Hunting and trapping are important occupations in the northern regions, along with reindeer herding. The U.S.S.R. has approximately two million reindeer, four-fifths of the total world population of that animal. Herds of reindeer are still moved back and forth between the northern taiga region and the tundra, according to the season, to feed on natural grasses. Most, however, are now kept on farms, where they are fed hay and other foods.

The Taiga

There is some farming in cleared areas in the taiga region. This is especially the case in the Yakut province along the Lena and other rivers. Summers are brief, but they are warm. Oats, rye, barley, and some wheat, along with vegeta-

A small Yakut bundles up.

bles, will ripen during the short growing season.

The vast taiga region covers a total of 2.8 million sq. miles (7.25 million sq. km). Much of the timber cut there each year is used for fuel. The remainder provides jobs for several million people who are connected with such industries or construction, furniture making, paper, and wood products.

Farming

Wheat, rye, and oats are grown on short-grass steppe land east of the Ural Mountains. Here, though, results are chancy. Rainfall amounts to only about 20 inches (50 cm) per year in many places. It is also irregular, and a year or more of drought is always a possibility. In addition, the soil is light, and winds are strong. This adds to the danger of soil erosion once the short-grass region is plowed for crops. The region has long been used for grazing cattle and sheep, and some people believe that that might be the best use for it.

The natural vegetation zones of the steppe west of the Ural Mountains and the area that once was mainly hardwood forests make up the heartland of farming in the Soviet Union. In this area, the climate is kinder than east of the Urals. The growing season is longer, and precipitation in some places ranges to above 30 inches (75 cm) a year. These are great fields of wheat, rye, oats, barley, and sugar beets. Dairy and beef cattle, pigs, and chickens are the main farm animals. There is much "suburban farming" in areas near such large cities as Moscow and Kiev, where vegetables and dairy products are produced.

Cows are pastured outside the town of Suzdal, not far from Moscow.

The mild climate around the Black Sea has permitted the cultivation of fruit crops not viable elsewhere in the U.S.S.R. Moldavia (above) is famous as a wine-growing region.

Pockets of Mediterranean climate along the Black Sea yield many different farm products. This is an area of grapes, plums, apples, citrus fruits, and pears, along with vegetables. Because of its great vineyards, it is an important wine-producing area.

Irrigation is used to aid farming in many parts of the U.S.S.R. This is true, for example, along the Volga River. Dams have turned the Volga into a series of narrow lakes. Water is drawn off reservoirs and channeled to fields of crops.

In the dry regions of Soviet Central Asia, irrigation has been especially important. The Kara Kum Canal runs for 500 miles (805 km) across that desert from the Amu Darya River to Ashkabad. Water from the canal has made the desert bloom, especially with cotton and vegetables. Hay is grown there to feed herds of sheep.

Organization of Farming

The word *farming* usually makes one think of an individual family whose members work together on a certain area of land to grow crops. The family might use some of the crops itself, or sell all of them to earn income.

This is not the way farming works in the U.S.S.R. The national government closely controls farming. Thousands of government workers are involved in deciding what and how much to produce, where it should be sent to market, and at what prices. Plans made in Moscow are passed down to local government officials who are to see that they are followed. The government also carries out the building of dams and the digging of canals and other parts of irrigation projects as well as the production of fertilizer and farm machinery.

There are three types of farms in the Soviet Union. One is the collective, called kolkhozy. Another is the state farm, known as sovkhozy. The third consists of small plots of land that are more like gardens than farms. These are worked by individual families.

About one-third of the land in the U.S.S.R. is farmed by kolkhozy. There are about 26,000 altogether and each is about 16,000 acres (6,500 ha) in size. Up to 450 families live on each collective. Some live in small cottages, while others reside in apartment buildings built of concrete. The members of each collective elect a committee to run it. The committee decides on such things as the purchase of machinery and fertilizer and when to plant and harvest.

Families on kolkhozy are paid with a share of the crops produced. They may use the crops themselves or sell them to the government. The collective itself also sells to the government. The income is used to pay for seeds, equipment, and other expenses necessary to run the farm. Expenses also include taxes that each collective must pay to the government. If there is any cash left over, it is divided among the families of the collective. The amount of money a family receives depends on the amount and type of work the members do. This is measured in "labor-day" units.

State farms—sovkhozy—are "factories in the field." Workers on them, like those in factories, are paid wages that the government sets.

State farms take up about two-thirds of the farmland in the Soviet Union. There are approximately 22,000 of them and the average is about 42,000 acres (17,000 hectares) in size. Most sovkhozy concentrate on producing a single crop, such as wheat, oats, or cotton.

A state farm in the Rostov region. These "factories in the field" provide on-site housing for the workers they employ.

Many workers on state farms live in concrete apartment buildings, just like city workers do. Their communities have schools, shops, medical and day-care centers, and recreational facilities.

Workers on both collective and state farms may have small plots of land for their own use. These are usually little more than an acre in size. Families may grow vegetables, keep chickens or pigs, or concentrate on raising beef cattle, dairy cows, or sheep. Whatever the families earn from the sale of their products is theirs to keep.

These small plots only a tiny fraction of all the farmland in the U.S.S.R. Yet, they produce a great deal. For example, two-thirds of all the potatoes and one-third of all the meat, vegetables, and eggs grown in the Soviet Union come from individual plots.

Even though it has great areas of farmland, during many years the Soviet Union has not grown enough food to feed its people. Food, especially wheat, must be bought from other countries.

Farming everywhere is a risky business. Because of the climate, it is especially so in the Soviet Union. Over the years, there has

Onions for sale at a Siberian market. Although private growers use only five percent of Soviet farmland, they supply more than half the food consumed in the U.S.S.R.

been one bad crop year out of every three due to drought, too much moisture, or unusually cold weather. There is, however, an unexplained disparity between the higher productivity of private plots versus that of state-owned lands. The government continues to try to increase farm production. Some observers believe one way to do that would be to allow farm managers a greater voice in farm operations. Another way might be to increase the amount of land individual families may farm for their own benefit.

Resources for Industry

The Soviet government controls manufacturing just as it does farming. Government officials issue plans to factory managers about what kind and how many goods to produce, as well as where to sell them and at what price. The government also sets wages and salaries of factory workers. It also collects taxes on the income factories earn from the sale of products.

There are several industrial centers in the Soviet Union. The older ones are located in and around Moscow and Leningrad. Both areas have woodworking and metalworking plants, along with factories that manufacture textiles, electrical equipment, chemicals, and

A view of the cannery shop at the processing complex of a Soviet fishery.

machinery of all kinds. The city of Gorky, east of Moscow, is known as the center of Soviet automobile manufacturing.

Large coal fields are located in the Donets Basin of the Ukraine, north of the Black Sea. Nearby are the iron ore resources of Krivoi Rog. The chief iron and steel producing centers of that region are Dnepropetrovsk, Zaporozhe, and Donestsk. Kiev, the capital of the Ukrainian Republic, is also a great manufacturing center, as is Kharkov, east of Kiev.

The Ural Mountains are rich in minerals, especially iron ore. Magnitogorsk, in the Urals, has long been a center for the production of iron ore and iron and steel products. Coal, however, is lacking here. It is transported from the Kuznetsk Basin, 1,400 miles (2,240 km) further east, and from mines near Karaganda, 800 miles (1,280 km) southeast in the Kazahk Republic. The Kuznetsk Basin itself is also an important manufacturing area.

Great deposits of oil have been tapped on land along the western edge of the Caspian Sea, centered at the city of Baku. Oil is also pumped from wells in the sea itself, where huge platforms have been built to draw it out. Other large oil fields are found in the Ukraine and in the Ural Mountains region. The Lake Baikal region is also a source of oil, and that region has become a center for manufacturing, too.

One dam at Volgograd on the Volga River alone can produce 11.5 billion kilowatt hours of electrical power a year. In addition, the Soviet Union has built up to a dozen nuclear power plants. Even so, most power comes from burning coal or oil to produce steam that turns turbines to generate electricity.

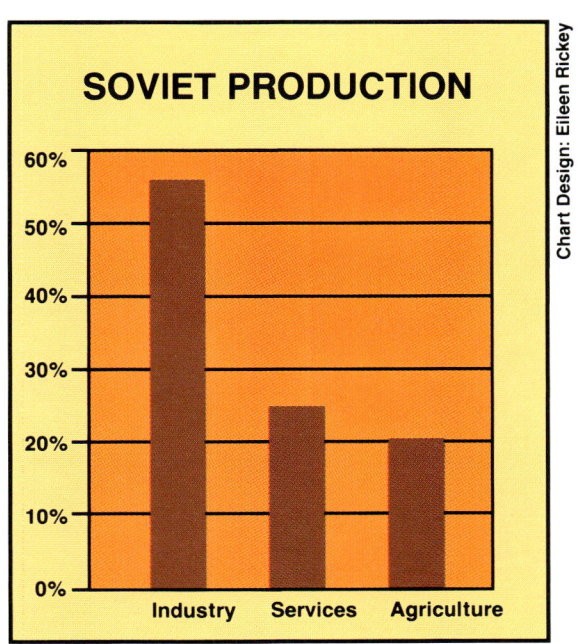

TBS/Reagan

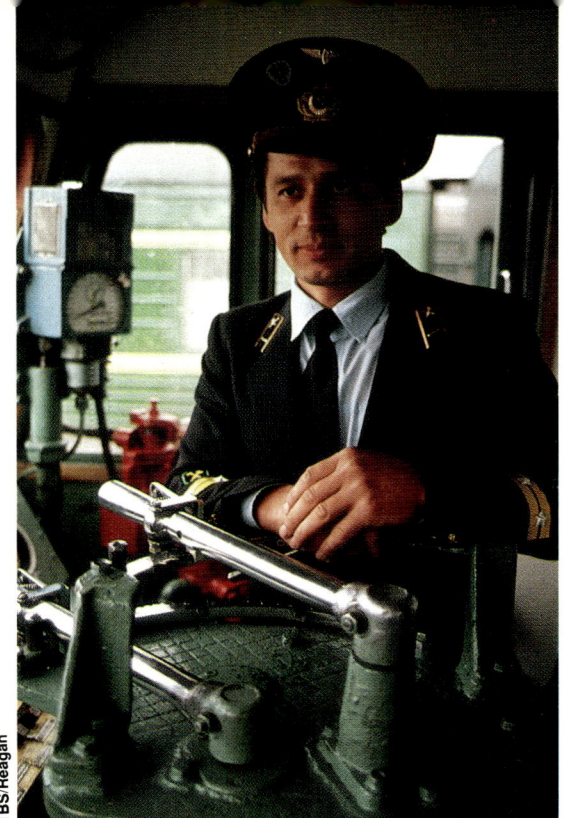

TRANSPORTATION

Railroad building in what is now the Soviet Union began in the 1800s. Rails linked such cities as Leningrad, Moscow, and Kiev, and fanned out from them.

The greatest rail project of all, the Trans-Siberian Railroad, was begun in 1891. It took more than twenty-five years to complete. A person can ride the Trans-Siberian from Moscow on a 5,600-mile (9,000-km), seven-day journey to

Views of the Trans-Siberian Railroad. About one-fifth of the route is electrified, the remainder having diesel locomotives.

TBS/Reagan

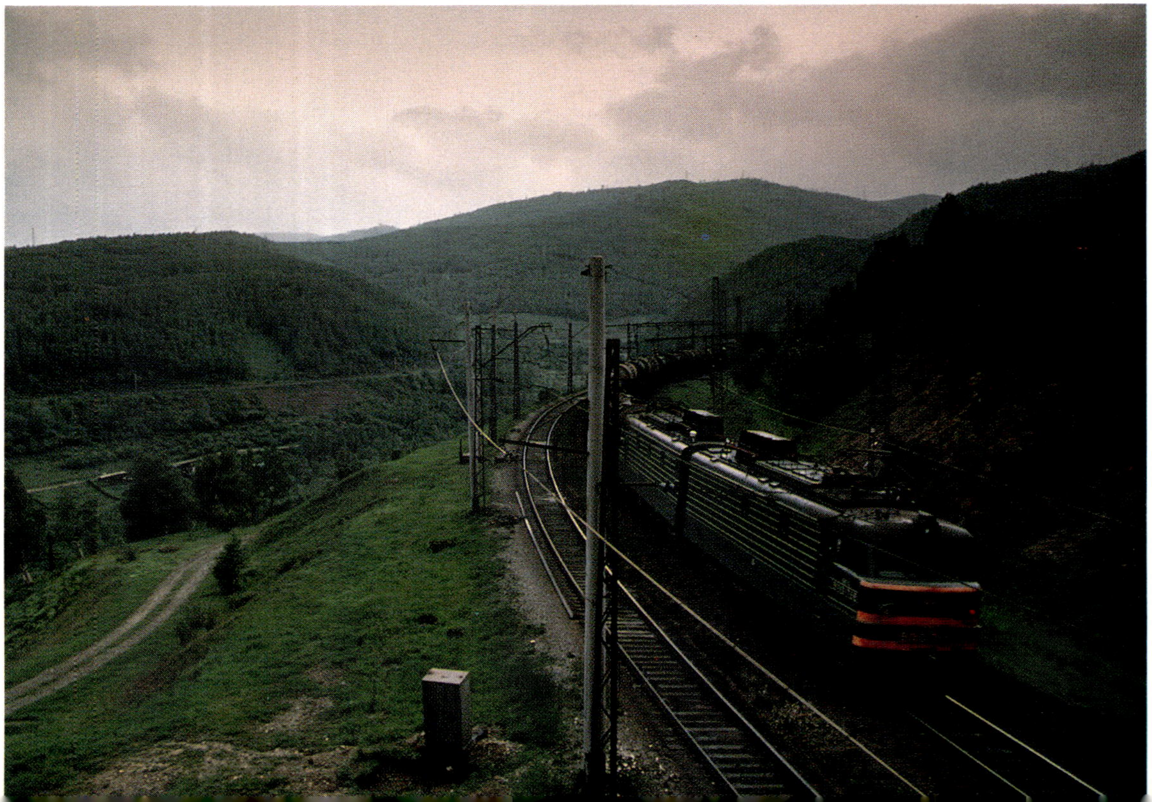

Major Ports, Airports, and Railroads of the U.S.S.R.

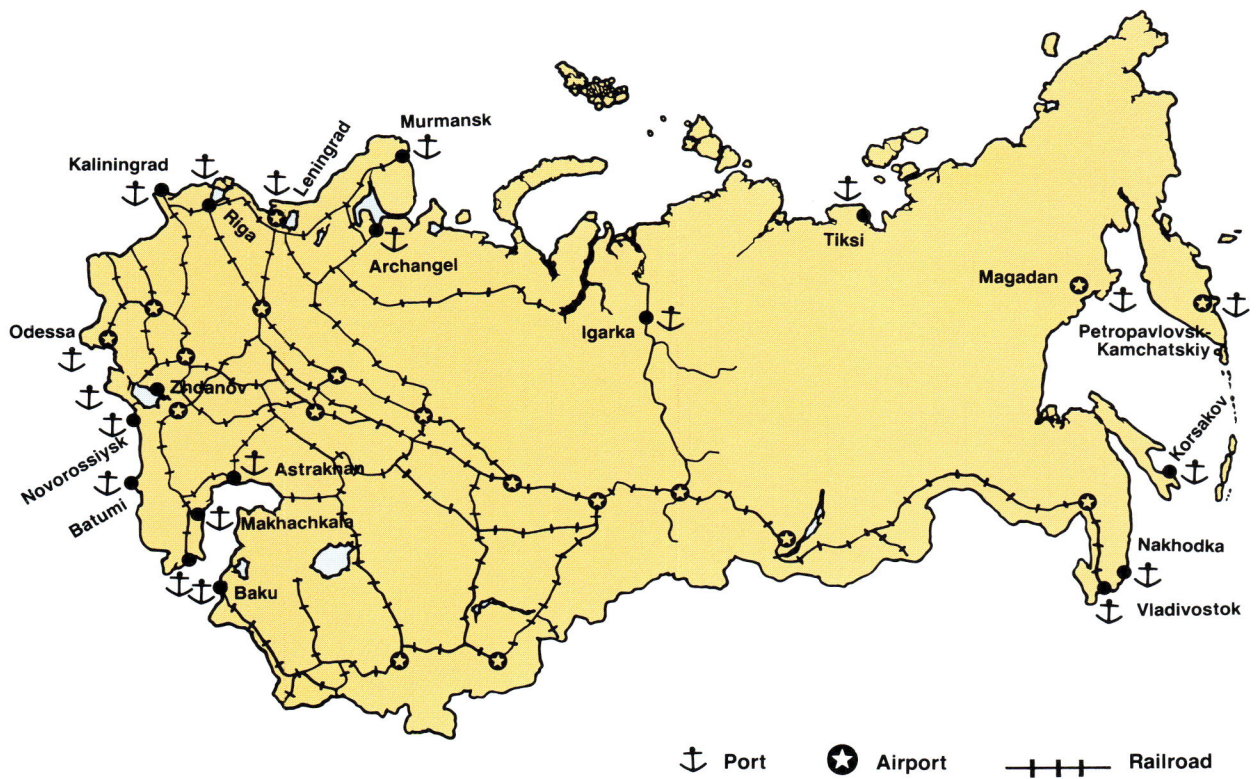

Vladivostok on the Pacific Ocean. Another line was built to connect Vladivostok to cities in the Ural Mountains region.

In recent years, yet another long railroad has been opened in southern Siberia. This is the Baikal-Amur Mainline, know as BAM. It runs from west of Lake Baikal to the Azur River, then to the Pacific. The BAM took many years to build and cost about $14 billion. A branch line of the BAM connects the area around Lake Baikal with the city of Yakutsk in east-central Siberia.

Altogether, the U.S.S.R. has nearly 90,000 miles (144,000 km) of railroads. A great deal of the nation's freight and nearly all the passenger traffic are carried by rail.

Freight hauling by railroad is especially important in the Soviet

Villagers rake by hand a dirt road in Irkutsk. Lack of adequate roads has created serious problems for the U.S.S.R. As much as a quarter of Soviet food being shipped to market spoils before it reaches its destination.

Union because of the lack of good, long-distance roads. In many places, there is a lack of hard rock near the surface of the land to serve as a firm base for concrete or asphalt roads. In addition, severe winters make it difficult to maintain roads. Most are dirt or covered with loose gravel, and they become muddy during rainy weather and spring thaws. There is little long-distance trucking in the Soviet Union.

There is little long-distance auto travel either. The Soviet Union has about 10 million cars, compared with about 125 million in the United States. The total length of highways, roads, and streets amounts to about 480,000 miles (770,000 km). This compares with 4 million miles (6.4 million km) in the United States.

Soviet citizens in cities do not depend nearly so much on cars as do citizens of such countries as the United States. Most city people get to and from work by train, bus, or subway. Leningrad, Moscow, and Kiev all have efficient, clean subways. Tashkent, the capital of the Kirghiz Republic in south-central Asia, also has a subway to serve its population of about two million.

Waterways are also useful as freight routes in the Soviet Union. Barge traffic is especially heavy on such rivers as the Volga. Canals connect it with the Moscow River, the Don, and the Baltic and White seas. River and canal traffic halts, of course, as waterways freeze during the winter months.

The Soviet Union has one airline—Aeroflot—which is owned by the government. Aeroflot furnishes passenger and freight service to all major Soviet cities and to more than eighty other countries.

An underground railway in Tashkent, Uzbekistan. Soviet urban mass-transit has made extensive use of such systems.

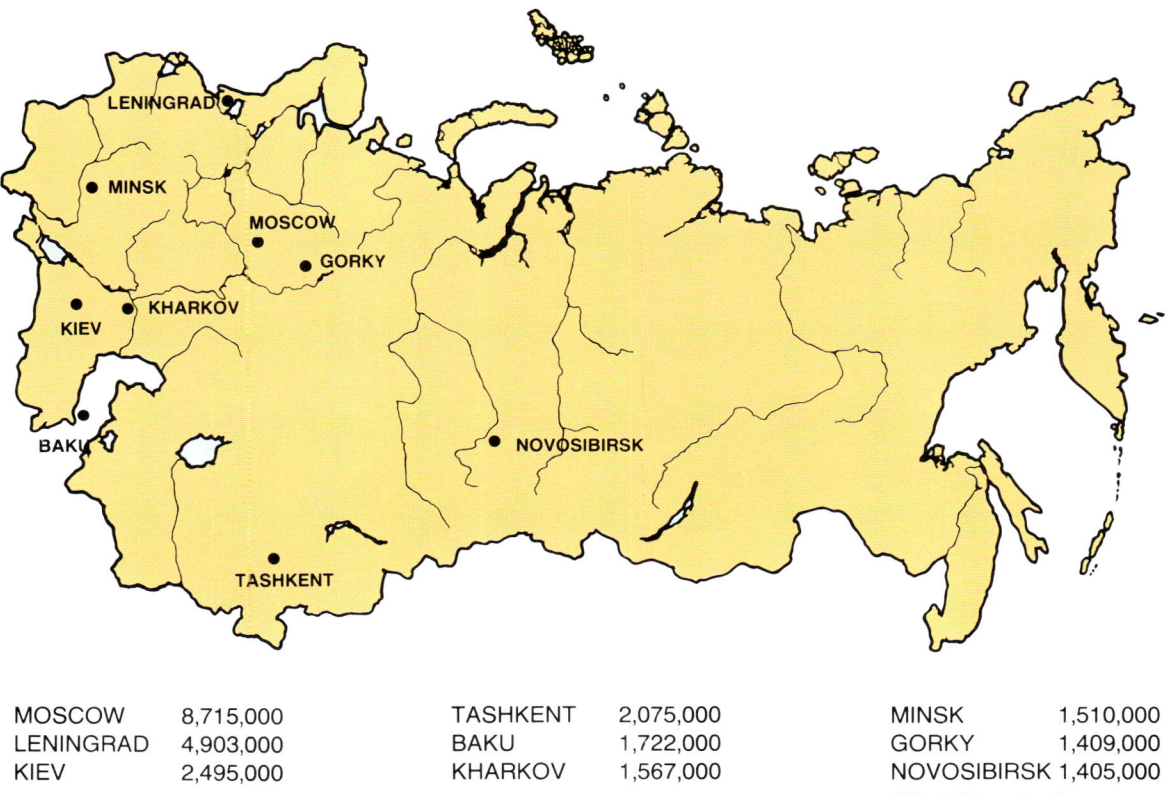

Populations of Some Major Soviet Cities*

MOSCOW	8,715,000	TASHKENT	2,075,000	MINSK	1,510,000
LENINGRAD	4,903,000	BAKU	1,722,000	GORKY	1,409,000
KIEV	2,495,000	KHARKOV	1,567,000	NOVOSIBIRSK	1,405,000

*Mid-1980s estimates

POPULATION

Slavic groups make up the majority of the 286 million people of the Soviet Union. Russians alone make up more than half the total population. Most Russians live in the western part of the country, but they are also scattered throughout the nation. Ukrainians are the next largest group, followed by Belorussians, who are also called White Russians. Ukrainians and Belorussians are concentrated in the western part of the U.S.S.R. Many people with Polish backgrounds also live in that region. To the north are the Baltic peoples of Latvia, Estonia, and Lithuania.

Large groups of Turkic peoples are found in Soviet Central Asia, between the Caspian Sea and the

Faces of the many Soviet ethnic peoples are visible on this crowded street in Siberia.

Soviet cities retain the distinctive architectures of their many historic periods. Above is the Baltic port city of Riga. Moscow, the Soviet capital, is at right.

border with China. Among them are Uzbeks, Kazakhs, Kirghiz, and Turkmen. Azerbaijanis occupy the Caucasus Mountain area, along with Armenians and Georgians. Many Bashirs, Chuvash, and Tartar peoples live in the Volga River valley.

Population growth has been greatest among non-Slavic people, especially those who live in Soviet Central Asia. Some observers believe that by the beginning of the 2000s, the peoples of that region will make up more than one-fifth of the nation's total population. If so, the Russian portion of the population will drop to less than one-half.

Until only about thirty years ago, more than one-half of the Soviet population lived on farms or in small villages. Since then,

the reverse has been true—more than half live in urban areas, in cities and suburbs. Moscow, with a population of more than eight million, continues to grow, as do other western cities such as Leningrad, Kiev, and Kharkov. Cities of the east and far south, such as Sverdlovsk, Novosibirsk, and Tashkent, all of which have populations of more than one million people, also continue to grow.

A Chronology of the Soviet Union

800s The Viking Rurik is the first ruler of Russia. The first Russian state is established. Kiev is the center of government.

988 Vladimir I introduces Christianity to Russia. The Cryllic alphabet is adopted.

1200s Russia comes under Mongol rule.

Late 1400s Czar Ivan III ends Mongol rule.

1547 Ivan IV becomes first crowned czar.

1613 After ten years of civil war Michael Romanov becomes czar. His family will rule Russia for three hundred years.

1703 Peter I founds St. Petersburg; he tries to bring Western ways to Russia.

1812 Napoleon invades Russia with an army of 600,000 but is badly defeated.

1825 Some nobles and army officers demand rule by law. Members of this "Decembrist Revolt" are hanged by Nicholas I.

1861 Alexander II frees the serfs. Some towns gain self-government.

1905 Russo-Japanese war is fought, and Russia is defeated. Nicholas II is forced to establish representative government.

1914-1917 With France and England, Russia enters World War I against Germany and Austria-Hungary.

1917 Revolt forces Nicholas I out. Lenin becomes dictator. The Soviet Union withdraws from World War I.

1918-1921 Civil war with anti-Communists rages.

1922 The Union of Soviet Socialist Republics is established.

1924 Lenin dies, and Joseph Stalin gains power over the Communist party.

1929 Stalin becomes dictator.

1939 World War II begins in Europe.

1941 The Soviet Union enters the war on the side of the allies after being attacked by Germany.

Late 1940s In the years following World War II, the Soviet Union takes over Poland, Hungary, Yugoslavia, and other eastern countries, creating the Iron Curtain.

1953 Joseph Stalin dies and Nikita Khrushchev comes to power.

1956 Khrushchev criticizes Stalin's methods of ruling and announces the philosophy of peaceful coexistence with the West.

1957 The Soviet Union launches *Sputnik I*, the first spaceship to orbit the earth.

1960 The Soviet Union brings down a U.S. intelligence-gathering plane.

1961 Yuri Gagarin becomes the first person to orbit the earth.

1962 Soviet missile bases are discovered in Cuba, causing tension between the United States and the Soviet Union. The bases are later removed.

1964 Khrushchev is forced to retire. Leonid Brezhnev becomes head of the Communist party.

1980-1985 Four heads of government die.

1985 Mikhail Gorbachev becomes head of the Communist party. He announces great changes in the Soviet Union in the form of *glasnost* (openness) and *perestroika* (making over).

1985-1988 Gorbachev and President Ronald Reagan meet five times. The Soviet Union and the United States agree to reduce the number of their nuclear weapons.

1989 The Soviet Union withdraws its troops from Afghanistan and also agrees to cut its armed forces by 500,000.

Map of the Soviet Republics

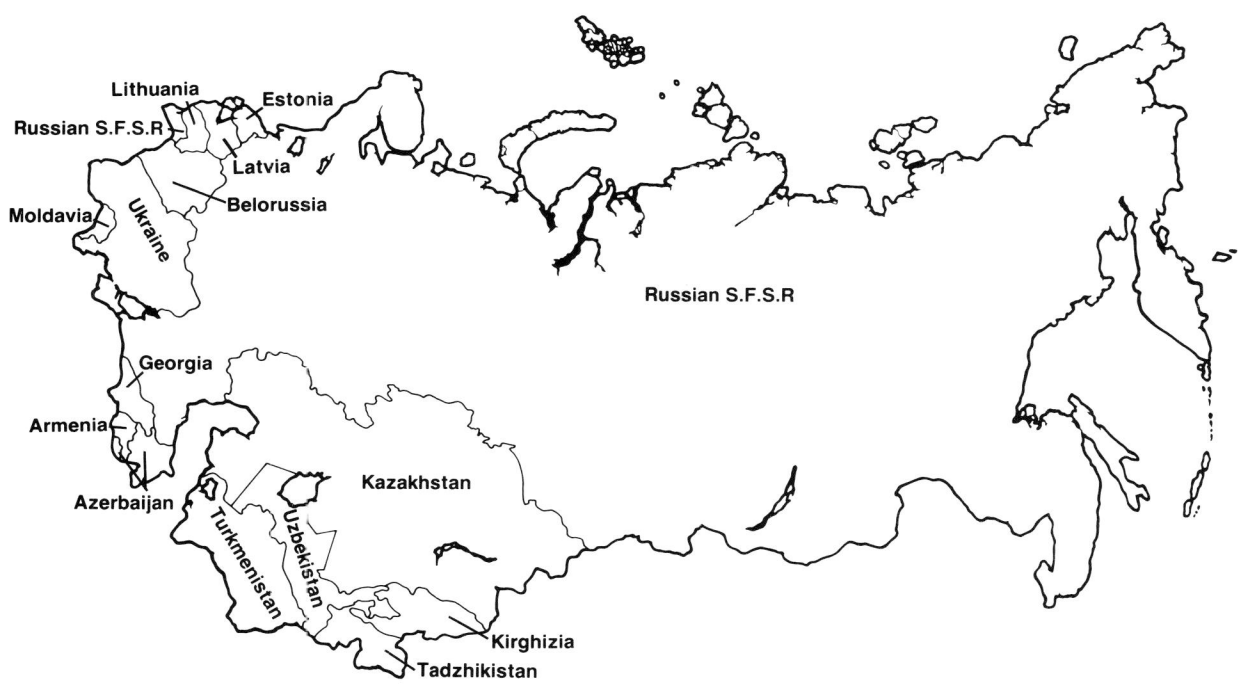

REPUBLIC	POPULATION*	CAPITAL
Russian S.F.S.R.	144,000,000	Moscow
Ukraine	50,900,000	Kiev
Uzbekistan	18,500,000	Tashkent
Kazakhstan	16,000,000	Alma-Ata
Belorussia	10,000,000	Minsk
Azerbaijan	6,700,000	Baku
Georgia	5,270,000	Tbilisi
Tadzhikistan	4,600,000	Dushanbe
Moldavia	4,100,000	Kishinev
Kirghizia	4,000,000	Frunze
Lithuania	3,600,000	Vilnius
Armenia	3,345,000	Erevan
Turkmenistan	3,200,000	Ashkhadbad
Latvia	2,600,000	Riga
Estonia	1,542,000	Tallin

*Mid-1980s estimate

INDEX

Aeroflot, 41
animals, 21, 23
automobiles, 37, 40-41

Baikal-Amur Mainline railroad (BAM), 39
Busheyev, Georgyi, 6

Carpathian Mountains, 8, 10
Caspian Sea, 15
Caucasus Mountains, 8
Central Siberian Plateau, 12
chernozem, 24
climate, 16-19
climatic regions, 18-19
coal, 37
collective farm, 33, 34
continental climate, 18

deserts, 24-26
East Siberian Uplands, 13-14
European Plain, 8-10

farm, individual, 33, 34, 35
farming, 30-35
grains, 30
industry, 36-37

Kara Kum, 26
Kara Kum Canal, 32-33
Karagiye Depression, 15
kolkhozy, 33-34
Kyzyl Kum, 26

Lake Baikal, 12
land regions, 8-15

mountains, 8-10, 12, 15
Murmansk, 28-29

natural resources, 27-37
Norilsk, 29
oil, 37

permafrost, 21, 22
population, 6, 43-45
precipitation, 18-19, 22, 24, 31

reindeer, 30
rivers, 8, 10, 12

soil erosion, 31
Soviet Central Asia, 14-15
sovkhozy, 33
state farm, 33, 34
steppe, 24
subtropical (zone), 26-27
subways, 41
summer, 17, 18

taiga, 22-24, 30
Trans-Siberian Railroad, 38-39
transportation, 38-40
trees, 23, 24
tundra, 20-22, 28

Ural Mountains, 10-11
vegetation zones, 20-27
Volga River, 8, 10

waterways, 41
West Siberian Plain, 12
winter, 16, 17, 18

BRANDYWINE PUBLIC SCHOOLS
Elementary Library
2428 S. 13th Street
Niles, MI 49120